JUNIOR MONSTER SCOUTS

Pumpkin Party

By Joe McGee
Illustrated by Ethan Long

Ready-to-Read

Simon Spotlight
New York   Amsterdam/Antwerp   London
Toronto   Sydney/Melbourne   New Delhi

For gourd lovers everywhere. Gourd is a very fun word to say!
—J. M.

To Joan and Larry, pumpkin carvers for life
—E. L.

SIMON SPOTLIGHT
An imprint of Simon & Schuster Children's Publishing Division
1230 Avenue of the Americas, New York, New York 10020
For more than 100 years, Simon & Schuster has championed authors and the stories they create.
By respecting the copyright of an author's intellectual property, you enable Simon & Schuster and the author to continue publishing exceptional books for years to come. We thank you for supporting the author's copyright by purchasing an authorized edition of this book.
No amount of this book may be reproduced or stored in any format, nor may it be uploaded to any website, database, language-learning model, or other repository, retrieval, or artificial intelligence system without express permission. All rights reserved. Inquiries may be directed to Simon & Schuster, 1230 Avenue of the Americas, New York, NY 10020 or permissions@simonandschuster.com.
This Simon Spotlight edition July 2025
Text © 2025 by Joseph McGee
Illustrations © 2025 by Ethan Long
All rights reserved, including the right of reproduction in whole or in part in any form.
SIMON SPOTLIGHT, READY-TO-READ, and colophon are registered trademarks of Simon & Schuster, LLC.
For information about special discounts for bulk purchases, please contact Simon & Schuster Special Sales at 1-866-506-1949 or business@simonandschuster.com.
Simon & Schuster strongly believes in freedom of expression and stands against censorship in all its forms. For more information, visit BooksBelong.com.
The Simon & Schuster Speakers Bureau can bring authors to your live event. For more information or to book an event contact the Simon & Schuster Speakers Bureau at 1-866-248-3049 or visit our website at www.simonspeakers.com.
Manufactured in the United States of America 0525 LAK
10 9 8 7 6 5 4 3 2 1
CIP data for this book is available from the Library of Congress.
ISBN 9781665970211 (hc)
ISBN 9781665970204 (pbk)
ISBN 9781665970228 (ebook)

Vampyra, Franky, and Wolfy were very excited.
It was Halloween at Castle Dracula, and they were going to have a party!

"We can dress up in costumes," said Franky.

"And play games," said Wolfy.

"And have a jack-o'-lantern-carving contest!" Vampyra said.

Franky and Wolfy thought that a jack-o'-lantern-carving contest was a very good idea.
They could make fun faces or designs, and they could put small lights inside the pumpkins.

They could even put
the carved pumpkins in front of the
castle for trick-or-treaters to see!
But first they needed some pumpkins.

Franky, Vampyra, and Wolfy marched to the pumpkin patch next to the castle.

"Look at all these pumpkins,"
said Vampyra.
"I don't even know where to start,"
said Wolfy.
"I'm going to find the biggest one!"
Franky said.

The patch was filled with pumpkins of every shape and size. There were big pumpkins and small pumpkins.

There were round pumpkins
and oval pumpkins.

There were even smooth pumpkins
and bumpy pumpkins.

Now all they had to do was find
the right pumpkins to carve.

Vampyra found a short, wide pumpkin.
She was going to carve a bat.
Franky found a large, oval pumpkin.
He was going to carve Castle Dracula.
Wolfy found a nice, round pumpkin.
He was going to carve a wolf
howling at the moon.

But when they went to pick their pumpkins, the pumpkins popped up and moved away.

"What's the big idea?"
asked the wide pumpkin.
"Yeah," said the oval pumpkin.
"We were resting here!"
"Are you trying to pick us?"
asked the round pumpkin.

Wolfy shrugged. "Well . . . yeah?"
"We're having a party," said Franky.
"With a jack-o'-lantern-carving contest," Vampyra said.
"A WHAT?!" the pumpkins all shouted.

They shook their vines and rolled in circles. They could not believe what they had just heard.

A jack-o'-lantern-carving contest?
That meant carving tools.
That meant little glowing
lights twinkling inside them.
No way.

The pumpkins were just fine
with staying the way they were.

The pumpkins moved
even farther away.
"You're just going to have
to have your party without us,"
said the wide pumpkin.

"Yeah," said the round pumpkin.
"We refuse."
"Now please leave our pumpkin patch," said the oval pumpkin.
Wolfy, Franky, and Vampyra were very surprised.

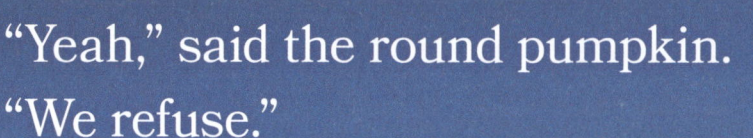

They had not expected this at all. Sure, they thought, they could still have their party, but they had really been looking forward to decorating pumpkins.

The moon slipped out from behind the clouds. It cast a bright image of the moon on the oval pumpkin.
"Look!" said Wolfy.
He pointed at the moon on the oval pumpkin's orange body.

"That's it," said Vampyra.
"We can paint our designs on our pumpkins. We don't need to carve."
"We can invite the pumpkins to our party and have a pageant!" said Franky.

The pumpkins stood together in the middle of the patch. "What are you three whispering about?" asked the round pumpkin.

"We were wondering if you'd like to come to our Halloween party," said Vampyra.

"We could have a pumpkin pageant!" said Franky.

"The entire patch is invited!" said Wolfy.

He leaned back and howled at the moon.

The pumpkins put their stems together and talked.
They thought the party sounded fun.
A pageant meant that they would each get a colorful design painted on them.

This was going to be a Halloween party to remember!

"We're in!" said the wide pumpkin.

"Party time!" said the oval pumpkin.

Vampyra, Franky, and Wolfy led the way back to Castle Dracula with the whole patch of excited pumpkins bouncing and rolling behind them.

When the pumpkins arrived at the main hall of Castle Dracula, they couldn't believe their eyes!
"Wow!" said the round pumpkin.
"Look at these decorations!"

Wolfy, Vampyra, and Franky put on their costumes while the pumpkins picked out paint and brushes.

The skeleton band played wonderful music while the ghosts and ghouls all danced.

Vampyra painted three bats flying on her pumpkin.
Wolfy painted a wolf howling at the moon on his pumpkin.
And Franky painted Castle Dracula on his.

All the other pumpkins joined in. They used their vines to hold their paintbrushes and took turns painting cats, witches, spiderwebs, and silly faces on one another.

When it was time for the pageant,
the pumpkins all lined up
to show off their art.
All the designs were so wonderful,
nobody could decide on a winner.

"We're all winners!" Franky said.
"What a fun party!" said Vampyra.
She twirled around with her pumpkin.
"Happy Halloween!" howled Wolfy.
"Happy Halloween!" said the very happy pumpkins.